www.enchantedlion.com

First Reprint Edition published in 2018 by Enchanted Lion Books,
67 West Street, 317A, Brooklyn, New York 11222
Copyright © 1956 by Remi Charlip
Rights arranged with the John Wylie Agency
Originally published in 1956 by William R. Scott Inc., New York
Production: Marc Drumwright
All rights reserved under International and Pan-American Copyright Conventions.
A CIP record is on file with the Library of Congress
ISBN: 978-1-59270-234-3
1 3 5 7 9 8 6 4 2

DRESS UP
AND LET'S HAVE A PARTY

WRITTEN AND ILLUSTRATED BY
REMY CHARLIP

ENCHANTED LION BOOKS
NEW YORK

Once while his mother was baking a cake,

John tried on the pots and pans.

He liked the way he looked all dressed up, and that gave him an idea.

So he called all his friends...

and then he watched and waited for the party to begin.

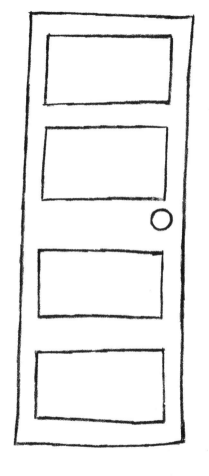

What would his friends wear when they came through the door?

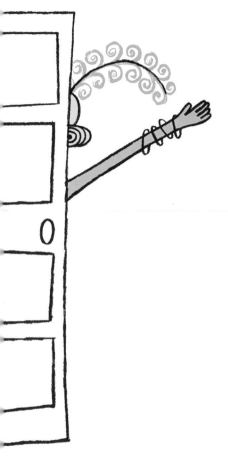

He knew that Marianne would come first.

She was always dressing up in her mother's clothes, and loved parties.

Hans didn't stop to make a costume.

But on the way he found a big box, so...

He came as a special delivery package.

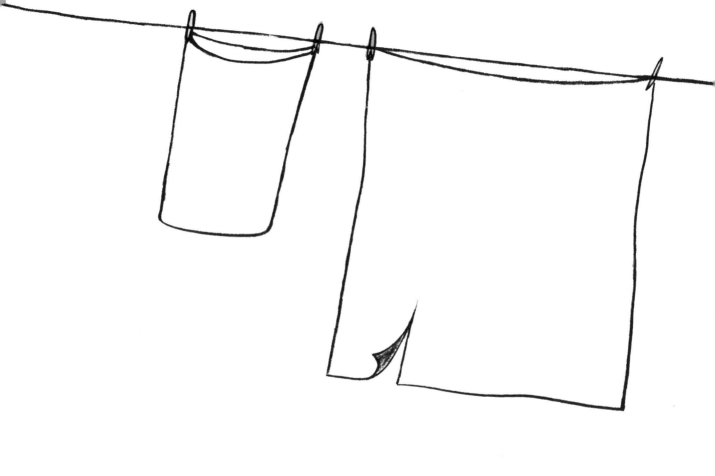

Charlie and Steve found a torn sheet and a pillow case...

and turned into mean ghosts.

Wearing an old lamp shade, Carol danced in as a ballerina.

Viola wanted to be a potato bug in a potato bag.

But Sue had nothing to wear, so they both got into a large skirt...

and came as close friends.

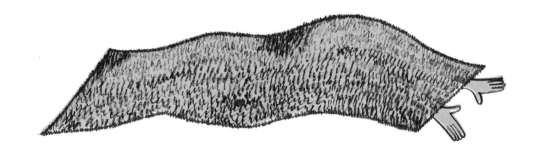

Under a blanket, Sarah crawled in as a mountain.

Ray was an elephant in his father's huge sweater.

Jenny never heard of a dress-up party, so she just wore a party dress.

Last came Vera as a meatball covered with spaghetti.

So John brought out the cake...

Then, while they were eating, they posed for a picture...

and when the cake was gone, they all went home.